A Darker Shadow

1

THE DARKNESS WITHIN

By AD Bane

Published by
AD Bane Publishing
British Columbia, Canada
Published in Canada, Printed in the USA
First Printing, 2018

ISBN 10: 0991833015
ISBN 13: 978-0991833016

To obtain additional copies of this book you can
find it available at Amazon. If you like it buy it.
Help support a struggling author!

Visit ADBane.com/news to keep up to date with
everything Mr. Bane is currently working on.

FOR THE LOST,
FOR THE SINNERS

A Darker Shadow

1 THE DARKNESS WITHIN

2 THE KNOCKER

3 RISEN DARKNESS

4 PRINCE OF DESTRUCTION

5 THE DEMON RUNNING

6 THE BITE OF THE WOLVEN

7 HE WHO WASN'T THERE

8 THE GIRL FROM CANCUN

9 TO ARBOUR

10 SUNFIRE

Look for these other chapters coming soon!

FOREWORD

A Darker Shadow began as this, a two thousand word short story about an exorcist with PTSD and a bad smoking habit. I could've just called it "Constantine" and never ever let it see the light of day for its blatant appropriation of an already-existing characterization. But since then it's morphed into a series of short stories about this guy who's intrigued my curious readers as much as myself. He isn't just my version of John Constantine anymore, he's become something else. He's found a place in the Universe beside the other characters who've imbedded themselves in my imaginings. And so here I'm bringing it into print with hopes of continuing Michael's story for years yet to come.

This is a story that relies heavily on religious concepts. While I don't believe in angels or demons and don't subscribe to a holy book, I find the notion fascinating. I have at times wondered how much of the unexplained can be explained by examining our own condition. Perhaps the paranormal is a state of the mind; perhaps Michael is fighting against his own delusions. Whichever you choose to believe, understand that this is a story of fiction first and foremost and should not be taken in any other way.

Finally, I realize this is hardly a good excuse for a book. 2000 words is barely even a short story. I've added filler pages to make this long-enough to print, and if I were you I'd feel taken advantage of. Please just keep in mind that my ultimate goal has always been to print these stories together in a regular book size, and the more of these you buy the closer I come to realizing that goal. Hopefully one day I'll be able to pay you back with a somewhat larger space in the world of these characters who've managed to turn my eventful life into something a little better.

And at that time Michael will arise, the great prince who fights for the children of your people: and there will be a time of trouble such as never was before . . .

- Daniel 12:1

And there was war in heaven: Michael and his angels fought against the dragon; and the dragon fought back with his angels.

- Revelation 12:7

THE DARKNESS WITHIN

He stood by the door without ringing the bell. His finger felt numb when he reached out to touch it, and he paused. The plastic button was faded and worn. It probably wouldn't even work. Those shabby, run-down apartments were much too familiar, though he'd buried the memories deep in his mind. The bell he remembered hadn't ever worked. But these weren't *his* apartments. He had to keep reminding himself that: not his but familiar just the same. He didn't want to go in, didn't want to know what memories he'd hidden, but knew he must.

The iron steps creaked beneath his weight, the weathered painted railing peeled beneath his fingers; and only just when he'd climbed the final step it come on him so suddenly. He stopped there with his hand to his head in vain to drive out the biting, gnawing ache that had

1

taken hold of him and to still the spiralling world in front of him. Just breathe, he told himself, calm and steady. And he did, for a minute or two. He stood there looking at the bell, that shabby old rundown bell on that shabby old run-down apartment. And he hated it.

The woman who answered the door was short and beautiful in her own dark way and spoke only something that wasn't quite English and wasn't quite Spanish. She muttered quite a few things he couldn't understand before she turned aside to let him pass. He stepped through the entrance corridor and into the kitchen. The lights were bad and made the paint look yellow. It smelled of mould and rot and other much worse things. He breathed it in and focused on the ache behind his eyes to keep the memories at bay.

The girl's mother was waiting for him, sitting at the table. She looked quite terrible. Her eyes were dim, and she haggard and worn from lack of sleep, her hair dishevelled and her dress all untidy and wrinkled about her. And it was with trembling hands and a quavering voice that she greeted him. "Mister Michael," she said through dry lips and a heavy accent, and she took his hand in hers. She could barely hold it, so violently was she shaking. And yet some semblance of a smile crossed her gaunt face, and that was quite reassuring.

"Miss Vasquez," he replied, and he shook her hand gently in his own and thought a woman so young and with so many years before her shouldn't have such rough and broken hands – rough and broken as his own.

"We're so grateful you could come," she said. "Was it any trouble?"

But he shook his head. "No." Not so much because it hadn't been any trouble but more so because she had much worse things to bother with than causing an interruption in his schedule. Not that he had a schedule.

"Where is it?" he asked.

At once her face clouded and her eyes were dark and troubled. Her hands were shaking again. "There," she said, and one trembling finger was outstretched to the shadowed hallway. "Last room on the right. Nikki is there already."

He'd only just paused, and he looked at her hard. "Did I not say that none should enter the room?" he asked.

"She hasn't left it," Miss Vasquez replied indifferently, and yet her eyes glistened and she put her face in her hands.

"Stay here," he said, and he took her by the shoulders gently. "No matter what you hear don't enter the room until I come out. Do you understand?"

She nodded through her hands and she didn't look at him.

The hallway was dark and the walls all in panel board. The dim incandescent light bulbs made no difference. It was a depressing sight. A cheerless place. And yet it was little surprise, the darkness. They loved it. Nor was it a surprise when the door stood only just ajar, and it creaked slightly when he pushed it aside.

Within, the room too was dim. The curtains were drawn, the bed unmade, things strewn about the floor. And the closet door stood open with the blackness inside glaring back out at him malevolently. Or so he thought at first. But it wasn't looking at him. Whatever was in there was focused on the girl.

She was young, cowering against the opposite wall beneath the curtained window, her face in her hands and her dark eyes watching from between her fingers. Her hair too was untidy as the room, her fingers stained, and she stared vacantly. She had seen him, he thought, and yet even when he stood in the doorway she didn't move. Not even her eyes, those great dark eyes that watched in horror and never seemed to see.

He shut the bedroom door, then the closet. Was no good to have that thing in the back watching. The door creaked when he closed it: it didn't want to shut, but he made it. And the girl looked at him then. "What was that?" she said, her voice weak with the same horror that held her empty eyes. He could barely hear her.

He didn't reply. He said instead, "Nikki?" and he stood in front of her to block the closet and what it hid. "Are you all right?" he asked.

Neither did she reply. She didn't remove her hands from her face, and her eyes didn't blink. "Are you an angel?" she asked weakly.

He shook his head. "No." He took her small hands in his great big ones and drew them away from her pale face. Her eyes were so dark and he didn't look in them. "Nikki," he said kindly, though he didn't smile. "It's all right. Why are you hiding?"

"I'm hiding from—" Her frail voice broke and she could say no more, though she pointed to the closet with a trembling hand and her eyes became wild with fright. "He watches me all the time!" she cried.

"Did he speak to you?" Michael asked, "Did he say anything at all?"

"He told me to come into the darkness," Nikki said. "He said he would rape me. He said he would kill me." She trembled violently and her eyes didn't moved, only her lips.

"It's all right," he said again. He looked her darkness in the eye and she back at him. She didn't blink.

"What's in there?" she asked, and the trembling ceased. Her hands were steady in his.

"It's a demon," he answered, and still he watched the shadow dance behind her eyes. It was angry. It hated him. It wanted him. It wanted for nothing more than to catch him in the dark and slit his throat.

"A demon?" she asked. "Can you make it go away?"

He didn't reply. He couldn't: his throat was dry. "Nikki," he said, "I need you to stay here and do not move, no matter what happens. And I need you to not scream either, no matter what. Can you do that?"

She said nothing. She only watched him vacantly, and still the darkness leapt behind her eyes. How it wanted him! He watched for a moment, wondering what it might be. But it wouldn't show itself. It never did, and there was really only one way to know for certain.

He arose and returned to the closet. The doors were still shut but he could feel it watching from within, waiting. It longed for him to come in, it longed to take hold of him in the shadows and strangle him, to wring his neck until he couldn't breathe anymore. And he knew how it felt, to hate so much.

He opened the doors and went in.

It came on him at once: the doors were hardly shut. It took him in claws that served only once purpose. It breathed on his neck, and such a hot, foul breath it was. The stench of it was in his lungs and he could feel its slimy hatred on his skin. And it spoke. "You cannot make me leave," it said. "You cannot make me leave this darkness. I will take her in the night and the shadows and I will destroy her."

He leaned against the panel board at the back of the closet. It rose to his head once more, gnawing and biting at his temple. He clutched at his scalp to calm the pain. It never worked. What he needed was four aspirin and a smoke. That would make it go away, give him some peace for the moment. He hated the pain. And that leering shadow. "Do you have a smoke?" he asked.

It laughed at him, and such a high cackling laugh as should've turned his insides out. Apparently that meant no.

"Have you not come to make me leave?" it asked.

"No," he said. Not yet.

Its scaly fingers reached over his shoulder. It was cold against his neck, and its touch on his breast was revolting.

It gave him a cigarette from the pocket of his jacket and he lit it in the dark.

"Then why have you come?" it asked.

He said nothing, not for awhile. He only drew on the cigarette and watched the embers glow red in the darkness. His breath drifted away from him to circle the shadows above his head. It made it slow and stupid.

At last he spoke. "What are you?" he asked, and he put out the cigarette. His head still throbbed but not so bad, and he could think clearly.

Again it laughed at him.

"You are nothing," he said, "just a slimy little part-blood."

"I am one of the Seven Sons of my Father!" it hissed at him angrily, and it took such a grip on him that he grimaced from the pain of its claws.

He was growing weary of its games by now. He longed for it to be over, for the thing in the shadows to be thrown back.

"By the Light, then, and show your wretched face to this world!" he replied, and he took hold of it and threw himself free of the closet and the darkness and the shadows within. On the floor he fell, and it on top of him. It cried in its horrible voice and screamed such a dreadful song as it clawed at him and tore at the bare floorboards. And Nikki did not say a word but covered her eyes and shook. So he held it fast and turned about and pushed it onto the floor. It was strong and it fought. "Who are you and to what purpose were you sent?" he demanded. But it only hissed and spat on the wood and the panel board. "Then back to the shadows," he cried, and he raised it up. It had grown weary in the light and was losing the fight. And so he took from his jacket a piece of cord and caught it about the neck like a garrotte and cast it back into the darkness of the closet. For a moment the shadows grew hot and burned as fire. The floor became ash and the walls turned to embers before his eyes. It screamed at him and clutched at the wood, drawing long scratches in the panels. But he kicked it in, holding it back by its neck. And then it was gone and the darkness returned and the shadows to haunt the living. He collapsed on the floor in front of the now empty closet, gasping for breath and drying the sweat from his forehead and wiping the grime from his hands.

It was a long time before he was able to stand again. "Nikki." His rough voice in the daylit curtained light of the small apartment bedroom. Her bright white eyes stared at him in horror from beneath her hands. "It's gone," he said. "It won't speak to you again."

"Ever?" she asked.

"Never," he said.

He could feel it again as the apartment door closed at his back. He clutched at his head, at that biting, gnawing pain in his temple. And the world began to turn once more. Just breathe, he told himself, calm and steady. And he did, for a minute or two. He stood there looking at the bell, that shabby old run-down bell on that shabby old run-down apartment. What he needed was four aspirin, he thought, and a cigarette.

About the Author

AD Bane is an avid enthusiast of science-fiction and fantasy. He's been dreaming and writing both since he first began to learn the art as a boy. He especially enjoys tales that stretch the confines of their genres and imagination.

AD Bane also enjoys philosophy and is fascinated by the machinery of the human condition. He writes stories such as this one both for pleasure and to present ideas that he believes can be difficult to grasp in reality. He's written many short stories, one novel, and is working on more, including a direct sequel to his first printed novel, Beyond the Wasteland.

You can find all his work available at Amazon and ADBane.com. You can also go to adbane.com/news for blog updates on what he's working on next!

BEYOND THE WASTELAND

A novel

By AD Bane

"It came from the east and went into the west with a rustle of the prairie grass and a cry of the rails that lasted on the wind, even until it was well beyond the next hill."

"It was a demon-train, Tucker, an evil thing if ever I saw one . . . and I intend to catch it."

Paperback and e-book now available at Amazon.ca and Amazon.com!